My Special Pet
by Heykid!

This book is dedicated to all the families that have supported our endeavors through the years...

Thank you,

Leigh, Joe, and Jack

I've got a special pet,
not like any in the world.
He has a horn on his head,
and his toes and tail are curled.

He's got scales on the side
and blubber underneath.
He has armor on his back
and you should see his pointy teeth.

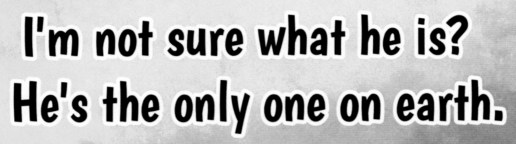

I'm not sure what he is?
He's the only one on earth.

He weighs 800 pounds,
weighed 250 at his birth.

He's part
dinosaur...

part
hippopotamus...

part
rhinoceros...

He's...a dinoptasaurus!

He is always hungry,
eats tons of plants and trees.

He is very loving,
likes me to pet
his head.

He would like to sleep with me but can't fit in my bed.

Our house is
too small for him,
it's hard to get around.

When he moves
from room to room,
he knocks things to the ground!

He makes funny noises, it's like a growl or roar!?

It's hard to sleep at night because all we do is hear him snore. zzzzz

He's part dinosaur...

part hippopotamus...

part rhinoceros...

He's...
a hipnosataurmus!

I'm very glad to have him.
I'm lucky as can be.

All the kids
at school
wish they could
have a pet like me!

He tries to sit in my lap
and likes to go on walks.

We get the ladder out to
help him with his
shoes and socks.

If you ever have the time
you should come on out
and meet him,

but not
between 3 and 6
because that is when we feed him.

When you finally make it over,
we might give you
a quiz...

He's part dinosaur...

part hippopotamus...

part rhinoceros...

Made in the USA
Monee, IL
16 December 2019